*For Carol —
Thank you!*

VERONICA, DAUGHTER

Prose & Poetry

Robert S. Hummel

authorHOUSE®

AuthorHouse™
1663 Liberty Drive
Bloomington, IN 47403
www.authorhouse.com
Phone: 1-800-839-8640

© 2014 Robert S. Hummel. All rights reserved.

Titles set in Palatino Linotype, designed by Hermann Zapf
Text set in Plantagenet Cherokee, designed by Sequoyah

Cover photographs by Robert S. Hummel
Author photograph by Christian Cassidy-Amstutz

No part of this book may be reproduced, stored in
a retrieval system, or transmitted by any means
without the written permission of the author.

Published by AuthorHouse   05/07/2014

ISBN: 978-1-4969-1111-7 (sc)
ISBN: 978-1-4969-1110-0 (e)

Any people depicted in stock imagery provided by Thinkstock are models,
and such images are being used for illustrative purposes only.
Certain stock imagery © Thinkstock.

This book is printed on acid-free paper.

Because of the dynamic nature of the Internet, any web addresses or
links contained in this book may have changed since publication and
may no longer be valid. The views expressed in this work are solely those
of the author and do not necessarily reflect the views of the publisher,
and the publisher hereby disclaims any responsibility for them.

To
SVF
PMF
JLH

CONTENTS

- 1   Village, Age Nine
- 3   Forewarnings
- 5   Monhegan Summer
- 7   A Song for Sheila
- 9   Quarter to Nine
- 11   Subtractions
- 14   Baptism 1997
- 17   Corpus Christi
- 20   Land of Faces
- 21   A Thinning Man
- 22   The Hush of Damp Empty Streetways
- 26   A Greeting
- 27   We Grow in Infinitesimals
- 29   Anthracite
- 31   Gratitude Stop
- 33   Prophet Song
- 35   Hypothetical #3
- 39   Filmmaking
- 41   It's a Judgment
- 42   The Message They Took
- 44   Street Wash
- 49   Crystal Made Flesh

50	The Resolution Sequence
54	I Sleep with Spirits
56	Coverings
57	Theory of Light
59	The Pilgrim
63	Bedsheet Lament
64	Older Now
67	Axiom
71	Here My Mind
73	Sestina for a Plateau
75	Inheritance

Everything seems a clue, an oracle: the nighthawk overhead, the rising moon, the faint sound of a guitar.
> *Terrence Malick,* The Tree of Life
> *First Draft, dated 25 June 2007*

VILLAGE, AGE NINE

The boy is still walking among that hallowed human autumn; upon concrete that bends to tree roots, against fragmented canopies stained with the lingering maple leaves, among the hundred silent houses with front yards standing as designated borderlands. He stops to pluck two of the scores of fallen acorns from the withering grasses, thinking about how treeleaves are like fingerprints. Walking on, he rubs the smoothskinned seeds together: they keep his hand warm. The other hand is fingering a thread deep within the pocket of his woolen coat. A broad sort of silence endures among the faint breeze and its chill, save the calls of large demon-prophet birds left behind, the drone of the limestone churches streets away, and his own voice, a high harmonium a hundred years closer to its first sound, pumped by an unseen hand, large against his little pale figure, which is moving slowly now towards the shrunken perspective of that minor turn in the road, named for a tree like the others. This street—now devoid of the dayworkmen of summer, toiling against plant odor and intermittent shade, men with their engines and bright shirts, with their monkish way of moving in time with the task—seems a crystalline preservation of the dead, an embalmment of the neighborhood. Yet it yields a certain comfort, a sensation of liberty, ownership: he is not the owner, but exists as a treasured property of the space itself, or whatever solemn heart tends to it. He imagines a girl from some centuries past spinning the atmosphere above him like an alchemist. He wants to walk with her. This is all he wants. Lonely, lonely—muttering he repeats this to puncture his own silence. He cuts through the doctor's backyard after the curve, as his mother had done long before he was brought to breathe this cold near-winter air, the air of this very village, and crosses the gray alleyway towards the home of his grandparents, that temple that brought greater comfort than seemed possible for him or anyone else to cultivate. Towards the doorway, past ivy and wrought-iron, he goes on.

FOREWARNINGS

I've anointed a bishop to address all matters of forever
As spelled out in covert notebooks of skin,
As used in any context whatsoever.
I've drafted pig's blood letters to a Pope
With my unqualified right hand
Demanding the abolition of the clock face.
I'm a festival of campfires alight down Hudson Street
And it's a beautiful evening for love.

I flagellate for silence tonight
Lighting flameless candles for hornet repulsion
For solitude attraction
For crystal forest seduction
For running storm drain serenades
For you, for me, for me, for you.
I peel the bandages away from my throbbing backskin
And it's a quiet evening for love.

My granite fountain spring is for drinking;
Its nectar slides through a single copper-gold pipe
And a lone disciple tends to its longing.

It is awash in holiness, says an inscription, in Greek
Along its sculpted rigid surface.
It sends pulses along the concrete, through
    aqueducts.
Oh drinkers, visit me in my eternity, I say
And it's a soaking evening for love.

I choked when the sea spat me to shore
But now I suck the air of bedrooms once more
As you dry me with your amber hair
And refill my glass of celluloid brandy.
Dizzy, your skin takes in my hummingbird arms
And I scrutinize the chemical taint of aroma—
It lingers upon your neck and collarbone
And it's a spotless evening for love.

Incensed dampness before this, and now we lie
Softlit against a growing fever of shaded
    synesthesia;
We twine like pulp at rest beneath trunkmoss
Sunken trees with earth-encumbered wasps' nests
The plushest void of cancer memory expunged—
Here we are, and somehow and so long
And I don't think I've ever slept so comfortably.
And it's a beautiful morning for love.

MONHEGAN SUMMER
After Hopper

There was a painting I did
When I was twenty-seven
(Six years ago)
Of Natalya, whom I had met
In a summer city bar.

Box of warm pale yellow
On the seagreen floor
And your black bunned hair
Six inches above your pale bareness and fur,
Also black. The white shirt was too stuffy.

It's sitting at my mother's house
In my childhood closet
Covered in a pillowcase
That's been stained by the oil leaks
From my growing head.

For whom, then, was the sorry thing made?
For years I was sorry I had it around
Because I was sorry to think of you

In your deep trance of love with someone
Certainly older and wealthier than I.

Maybe it's for the people of this fair island to see,
Your contortion, your waist, the sheet trapped
    under your bum.
They're the kind of people who would understand,
We're the kind who would mistake it for holiness.
There are few human idols twelve nautical miles
    from shore.

I dumped the city after four years of melting myself
In the hopes that I could be a new, softer color
Among the hard lonelies of the sidewalks.
O Monhegan, your tiny body catches mine—
Green, such green, and sapphire blue.

Seventy-five inhabitants, to whom I've spoken
    less than seventy words in all.
Not nearly five square miles, yet space enough
    for losing,
Hiding things like pillowcased memories.
I haven't met a girl here, in case you wondered
Though the sea is sucking through my door,
    through all my nights.

A SONG FOR SHEILA

He kissed where she'd asked him
She shuddered, she sighed
She led him to where the holy could hide
He moved and his mouth then gave birth to a word
She replied with a sound like the call of a bird.

When touched, she would tremble
If kissed, she would die
He tugged at her ankle as she smiled on high
He tried to reteach all the things he had learned
She just made a sound like the call of a bird.

He knew he'd remember
At least he would try
Her bare silhouette on a blue-darkened sky
And fondly the high song of love he had heard
When she made that sweet sound like the call of
    a bird.

When faced with her traces
He'd smother his cry
She'd appear as a face in the crowds that go by

He stopped at the corner, his vision now blurred
He heard it so distant, the call of a bird.

She told him, "Now Robert,"
In a timbre so high
"I belong to my whimsy, I'm given to fly."
She kissed and she flew. City crowds overheard
Her royal departure, the call of a bird.

QUARTER TO NINE
After Basinski

I can suck the dust from videotape
The way I suck building dust through the middle dawn.
They are twinned together, the National Secret Grief
And the International Secret Hate.
I demand that we demand—but the glory bleeds out
Before it can breathe the dusty air abound.
Instead, we dream of placid blue dreams—
Like turbulence we quiver at the missing heroes.
Heroes, I wish I could see your luscious cardstock wings:
I wish I could see what you wrote on them,
All those lipsmacking passages I draw now like an amoeba sketch
With metastatic ink that hazards my familiar image of you,
Each one of you.
Your destruction resounds in symphonic highs
My destruction resounds in empty clicks
Resound! Resound! Rejoice Almighty,

For they've shifted the architecture of a
   generation,
Of an entire city full of generations.
Our Judas apathy rests a dozen years, belly full.
The National Secret Grief cannot be reached for
   comment.
Meanwhile, three thousand are bleached from a
   Manhattan stain
And they leave behind a sarcophagus scent
That sticks like gasoline to the dust.

SUBTRACTIONS

IV
The nomad lovers walk at midnight and half
Aglow with the shrinking windows' glow;
Here is the beating heart of youth itself
Confined to a light-string room.

I need scotch and candles, your golden blood.
I can see the hair on my chest in your irises.
I thought that only happened in movies.

J'aime prendre un verre, you say.
Our waists against the bed, I say

As we swan around like popstars.

III
Your fingernails address the envelope of backskin
Into which you've tucked the deeper organs,
Folded like sex cash in wrinkled abandon.
Here I cry, cry, cry like clockchimes.

Fluids as God-symbols spread all across the floor,
The stain of almighty. All you need of heaven
Is a clean bed, an alcove, the sun.

The leaking heart of love, glistening
Pumps it out. Out it comes.

Fringing, here, I lap it up.

II
Chelsea, I'll forever walk with you
Through that infinite dawn
Of our private Manhattan:
The roads are empty

And the sidewalks are freshly laid,
Shining, as if born asleep.
You in your coat

And me in mine; the sky forever pink
On our faces, catching reflections

From the polished glass.

I
The littlest girl sisters sit quietly:
One coughs, and the other
Holds her arm so close.
The subway flies.

If you have five, father lofts,
And take away three,
What do you have?

Sister whispers sunny day truths
Into sister's right-side ear

And you, next to me, feel a little bit warmer.

BAPTISM 1997

Like a switch of birch
He whistles as he cuts through time.
Small child, behind plain backs
At last relieved of the plain faces—
One had eyeglasses stretched over eyebrows,
    beyond.

Their figures are wide as the cows;
In their huddle, it looks like a pilgrimage to water
But out there is Mother. A second head
Pushes hers below, beneath.
This he sees through the crowdgaps.

It is enough to hold his arm,
Still his growing face ahead
As if that stare fixes itself upon twenty-two rose
    petals
Eddying in the creek.
He counts them one by one.
There is no such ruby among all the August brown.
He turns towards the line of cars, above the dirty
    bank,

Tree roots, a twisted tree,
Wondering if it was time to go.

The cows are skinny as people
And the tree roots suck liquid hellfire like a torch.
Her head lingers underwater
As the engines charge themselves to dissonance.
Strange chalky strains of factory color
Are mixing into creekwater in webs and spirals.
They trickle in through lips and make organs
    shine.
All the force of water shifts upstream at once.

You Know You Have Done Wrong, Boy:
Think Of The Bedsheets You'll Steal
The Women You'll Make Unholy
And The Way You'll Make Love Wait For You
In Empty Early Morning Waiting Rooms.
A Man Will Ask You Questions Of Your Hate
And You Will Have To Answer To All You Think.

You must
Smother
What makes you a man.
Learn to breathe
Underwater.

Mother
Why, why dip?
Listen, instead:
Whoosh
Whoosh
Whoosh
Goes the switch.

CORPUS CHRISTI

The great window, invitational, sticks as I move it.
Weak arms, atrophied, are snowed upon by
    flaking paint, eggshell white.
Come here, maybe we can get it open together.

Treeleaves coax and sing behind glass.
Do they peer through dirty raindrop eyes to me?
With hush I carve numbers and plans into green
    walls.

My weight on the floor creaks across structures.
    Cautious eyes look up.
Shaking, I brush away my pity as gray dust,
    floating,
I shift myself away in the hopes of much lighter
    footfall.

Awash in hum, I cage. Here, now, in spaces split
    from the same cell,
I inhabit the rooms of many, fraternal and alike,
    where poets drown
And imagine cardinal heartbeats in their hands.

I hang from taut wires, surging nerves
I play quiet music, I play awful songs.
I'm the one snowing on your dreams at night.

The pale hearts around me cling to gray garments.
I look: they've been long sanded, gradually, 'til smooth as palmskin.
I roll them in my hand, I stain them with my storm.

You are one of them, hovering with your wicked glow, bearing honey
But your baptisms are awkward, strained, and interrupted:
You leave, disappointed, with clumps of my hair.

What else do I have to give
Except that which is forcibly removed
And then forcibly refused?

Twenty-four years from now, I'll stand on shores harboring the dead,
My feet sinking. My hands grope for liberty, graze something dead.
Trash: the water littered with pages like skin.

The incantations of the dead.
Tall billows bring rain. I find the cardinal. It is
    half-buried, dead.

So take another mouthful
Of deep chemical hate
And watch the perfect days ream by
Like unread pages, filled with blocks of English.

LAND OF FACES

The lighteyed woman in the second row of the balcony
(ex-mother, single wife, onetime something someone)
Thinks of opera voices in an entirely new way, fresh
Since reading the prose of Anaïs Nin for the first time
Since school; since affairing with the cop outside
Working the nighttime beat; since revisiting the scene
Of the accident to look for a stain where the car-corpses
Had been; since dancing atop the dull breakings of the
Buckley record she used to make love to; since love;
Since breaking a promise, ceremoniously sharing her
First smoke in nine months with a young nurse named
Scott; since oncoming traffic and no median; since her
Parents' house fell into the sinkhole, at last; since a
Barbiturate dream of Western collapse; since some
Stranger at the bookstore asked if it was all right if he
Took her photograph. Since all of this, her ears had
Changed their hearing. The soprano's voice was cold
As a crystal, and the bass rose from the mouth like
An ashen snake from fire.

A THINNING MAN

A thinning man
In a herringbone suitjacket
Walks Tangiers.
When he thinks of home
He feels rainsparks.
The darkhaired woman on his hotel patio wants
    him to be happy.

Ahead, he can see
Against dustwhite day
The bloody bedsheet banner
Of a gypsy wedding.
Behind him rise the frightened shouts of the plaza.
Silence.

THE HUSH OF DAMP EMPTY STREETWAYS

They'd both had enough of that diner, the only one in town open to midnight. Market Street was dark enough by then that the light diffused from its spotty front windows cast a dull fluorescence across the patched pavement. Alden rubbed the print of his thumb up and down along the ribbed edge of the prefab table and recalled the time when he was seventeen and had sat in that corner table and plotted a beeline route behind the counter and to the register when he had wanted to knock the place off with nothing but a shop hammer taken from the back garage which had piled with detritus and was left alone enough those twenty years. He had never seen it clean.

Mr. Thorpe sat adjacent, not across, with a brown jacket and textured tie as if it were some time before today. Hair greasy and loose from the day's business at the stoneyard: two sales and the weeds were encroaching upon the merchandise deep in the cleared-out field. He'd met the kid outside the place, both of them chewing on bagged tobacco and never having a formal encounter before that very dusk, despite narrow odds at having spent all their time of living in this dense borough of less than two thousand, many too old to work and others out in the steep hills in bigger houses. They'd both lived in town since their births, thirty-two years apart and in identical fading rooms in the tiny hospital.

Thorpe paid the bill and stretched when he stood, while the other just shifted himself up and to the door. Later, in the man's old SUV out by the riverfront park, Alden fielded an offer to rob a bank, and accepted. The headlights didn't reach the water, and neither of them felt concerned by the fact that they were on. A late-night AM radio show discussed queer lights in the sky outside of Phoenix; three of them, three miles apart.

He didn't have a car, so he walked from his house past the closed Italian eatery on Center with its sign missing only one letter in the four years of vacancy. Once he had sat with his girl Laurie on the stoop of that place after Mr. Brucci packed away the equipment he couldn't sell at the public auction and left with it all in the bed of his truck.

They drank Yuengling from bottles and sang to a bum between fits of spiteful laughter.

He walked past the red doors of the Lutheran church and imagined the steeple toppling over onto his frame and the rowhomes across the street. When he reached the Common Bank branch in town, he had lost his focus and in ten minutes was dead on the sidewalk from two .40 caliber impacts that were meant to wound but ended up puncturing the spinal cord and passing through to burrow into the body of a nearby Ford. His head lay flat sideways as if asleep, facing two bootprints formed in the concrete, brimming with rainwater from the evening drizzle and lingering dampness. The deputy's apology was genuine, and unconsciously he thumbed the tight, damp spot where his hat pressed against his forehead. The money was returned.

Two nights before, on Sunday, Thorpe had driven out to the Adult Outlet to watch one of his favorite dancers, whom he then paid to fuck in his car an hour after he arrived. Two days after the robbery, he drove the thing off a cliff, where it somersaulted once and fell into the shallowing river.

Laurie had skipped town by this time, and now held a baby in her arms and her husband stepped through the back door from an afternoon at the shooting range, the faint smell of burnt powder on his hair. After he had gone back outside, she turned back to the child and put her nose, her lips to little Paulie's crown and inhaled. She pressed harder than usual. Then, the sound of the mower filled the house from the wet lawn of the dimming morning after death.

A GREETING

The salt grass is cut short, beneath the brush.
They scrub feet, left bare. They scrub deep.
And the pillars are rocks, pointed to the sky,
To darkness. And you in your white rags,
In your small craft of one, shrink.
There are sensations that do not germinate abroad.
So you are always a student of the dead.

Can you cultivate extinctions? Can you raise,
In your wordlessness, text from ash?
Can you compel the dead to read from it?
Fashion tools for yourself, even people.
In dreams you will glide across oceans
But nude you will walk this blessed island,
For you are not beneath the waters.

WE GROW IN INFINITESIMALS

Fibrous and strong,
You've been stretching so very long. Your tendrils,
Your nerve endings stand taller each day.
    Remark on how you notice
The growing distance between your emerald
    spirit and your ground.
Beneath it you sheathe your roots.
In the husk, bright orange somehow,
Is an infant, an inchworm, tucked behind
    translucent skin.
Did it grow too close? Was it resting from the light?
My incubator, my murderer, my finest embryo.
Can you stretch me any higher?

Hands are fuzzed with particulates. A lonely bee
    carries it on his fur.
I dare not disturb it. My knees grind at
    themselves, and I pull another
Handful of green. Pregnant drops of rain in my
    eye, suspended on summer skin.
Weed, you feed on me, but I am an animal. My
    scent hovers about my space

And my lover. She rests with legs pulled up, her
>body deep in perfuming grass.
Her face hides beneath earthen hair. An arm
>covers her breasts. The rain,
Standing still around her, bows before its gentlest
>touch.

I catch a whiff of myself. She reaches hand and
>eye to me. Others descend,
Dip away, even the sun. We're soaked. She
>sheathes me.
She could consume me if it would please her.
>Instead, she is a teacher.
I want her to reach up, past my stone face,
And into canopies.

Between my eyeline and the floating dust,
>invisible,
A barred window gives way to meadows and trees.
Horizons for us.

ANTHRACITE

Yes, we are a city
But we are unannounced by highway signs
And at night we share the same image
Of ten dozen silhouettes upon mountains of soot;
Piling it on, soot from below the ground.

"We," as if it were
The seven-thousand of us in a great huddle
Making our way down Chestnut together,
Clutching leatherbound books or children,
Efforting on, into the lightbound cold morning.

As if we could open what is closed,
As if we could tear into the earth for her riches
Once more, as if that would be enough to save us;
As if that could bring you to me, to my city.
Instead, I am alone. I dare not build around my
    hope.

Another dream:
A stone-frozen American Pompeii
Where the flames opened the road to spit
    skyward.

They build new roads around our petrified
 embers
As we sink our way into the ground, too heavy
 for smoke.

Here I dream,
Alone, and growing into fatherhood.

GRATITUDE STOP

These unintentionals are stacking up like a stack of rotten bananas, a boatful of them, carrying a neonate feeling of fear destined to grow up a prince and tear down walls and seas. Run and jump over yourself, lying prone along the otherwise empty pathway through the forest behind the towers. Sylvia Plath called, she wants her identity back. I called, I want the other house back. My kids, two daughters, run up the stairs of my building and stop in front of my door, run back down again. Their mother sent them on a plane by themselves and I'm pissed because they're definitely not old enough for something like that and I actually started heaving with anxiety as they shot across land for eight hours from Seattle to Montreal and I called their mother and couldn't even make myself angry, I just cried a little and told her that this wasn't the place I had in mind for myself, or for you. You said that I wasn't in control of you. You sighed something like It'll be okay and I didn't believe you for a second and you *knew* it, too, which is the worst part about it. I found the largest book you ever gave me and hit myself again and again on my face, creating a fold across the length of it from my big nose. Two minutes later I had a black eye, but I tell everyone a different story. I tell my daughters that daddy clocked himself good while he was dreaming about a boxing match, but now their eyes seem to shade me with even more pity than before (they're old enough now) and I know I fucked that one up. I haven't spoken more than 200 words today, so this is quite the dambreak. I remember a girl who wrote down how angry she was at me for my weakness. I remember making another girl cry. That was a long time ago. You should move into the house and be alone because you'll seem that much stronger in my eyes for it. I want to die in that house one day. I want to live there, anywhere but Montreal, now that I've settled down. I'm losing weight to spite people. I wanted to thank you for giving me that bed of yours for four months while I died and was resurrected by a personal Christ, but I don't think you touched me more than twice. Right. That's what this was supposed to be. Thank you. Thank you.

PROPHET SONG

You are a prophet, sweetheart
You sleep in silken clothes:
You bathe in cavern waterfalls
And write your cryptic prose
My trembling voice, all drowned in love
Cries once, and then it goes—
You are a prophet, sweetheart
You sleep in silken clothes.

You are a prophet, darling
You sculpt beautiful songs:
You sing to higher nature
You kiss away the wrongs
Oh, take my lonely spirit
It thinks that it belongs—
You are a prophet, darling
You sculpt beautiful songs.

You are a prophet, beautiful
You pray against my sin:
My hopeless grieving tendencies
The void of soul within
I'd prepare a sacred banquet

If I knew where to begin—
You are a prophet, beautiful
You pray against my sin.

You are a prophet, dearest
You've foreseen my eclipse:
You've seen my other women
A bottle to my lips
My sinking, broken body
The sand up to my hips—
You are a prophet, dearest
You've foreseen my eclipse.

You are a prophet, lover
I give myself to you:
My vault of adoration
My brimming glass of dew
Oh, seal the open wound of love
I've long tried to subdue—
You are a prophet, lover
I give myself to you.

HYPOTHETICAL #3

Christ the Tiger is asleep in a banana tree behind glass in a Berlin zoo. Why are we in Berlin, you ask, I don't really like it here. Christ sends me a look, which I return fearlessly, my trust breathing against the glass to test its sturdiness. Okay, I say. My eyes look up a little bit to meet yours: the tungsten light makes them translucent and amber in the second before you look away, at anything else. There's something trapped inside those eyes, and I want to breathe all over them to melt the membrane and reanimate it, whatever it is. I might be liberating something terrifying, some kind of unholy visionary death, but I don't mind because the melting process requires that we remove all of our clothes in a dark hotel room. I tell you this, and you say that it'll have to wait until we get to Paris. Paris again? We already drank all the champagne in that hotel, I say. We already alienated the room service waiter. The sheet slipped when I answered the door that one time. We'll go to a new hotel, you say. We'll go to Prague, I say. Compromise was Amsterdam. So now I'm carrying our bags down the grand old staircase of the hotel and giving the key—an actual key—back to Frau Rheingold at the desk, who again seems to forget that I don't speak a word of German. Danke, you say. Danke, I say as we go out the big iron door and into the street. Somehow the car takes us to Potsdamer Platz though I swear I told the driver to head somewhere else, like the airport, but you're out of the car already and I'm hustling out after you, gently dropping Euros on the seat for the large man driving. You smile at me, and lead the way as we walk towards side streets in a more modern district that reminds you of university days in the states. I was always good at finding the quiet bars there, where I could get a twenty-dollar New York strip and a glass of scotch and eventually the two would taste the same and I'd stop thinking about anything else, so remarkable was the flavor; like the beating, benevolent heart of forest topsoil, taken from a high hill that gives a view of two farmhouses in the distance where the greens are deep enough to sing with violins in echoes across the landscape. In the end, I have a beer and you have a full glass of red. There's something about watching you walk down city streets, I say. You smile; your mouth shrinks, and you look away, down at the wooden floor, up to the wooden table, then up to my wooden brown eyes and past them to the light of the wood-framed window, following it out to a man using an umbrella as a cane, walking swiftly past the storefront. He has a trenchcoat and a fedora, and you think that's the kind of absurd, anachronistic wonder that's keeping society from collapsing. I head, with a studied grace, over to the restroom just to look at myself in the mirror: the door is locked from the inside, and the cooked bourbon smell of propane is wafting in from the door out to the alleyway. A bald man walks past me with a look of stern inebriation and I hurry back to the table, where you sit and somehow know exactly what happened. Even I'm not sure what happened. My face feels like it's being projected onto a balloon, so you reach across and touch it with fingertips and suddenly I don't say or think a word. They're playing Wagner's Prelude to *Parsifal* for some reason, but I realize that maybe it's only in my head. The last time I heard it was when we were walking through Chelsea just before that snatch of rain drove us onto a covered stoop to kiss. After that I had to go five hours back to where I came from, where I rearranged my life and grew out a beard for the first time, thinking "God gave me this" even though I had been arguing against the idea of God all semester. A man at the airport has a Bethany Beach sweatshirt on and so we smile. He speaks to his lover in Spanish. So we smile. I'm sitting next to you as you cover me with your omnidirectional eyes, scanning the terminal but seeming always to rest on me. Your infinite periphery favors my strange unbearded face, gaunt and staring back at eyecorners, dipping down. You look sad until you're happy, an old-fashioned happiness that spreads like victory. Snap goes my old camera. The look on your face grows even further.

FILMMAKING
For KSF

I
The first soggy snowfall through the kitchen
    window.
I've collected it in a crystal vial, for later use
As your false movie teardrops.

I long to study the melt on your eyelash.
Instead, I have you clean broken glass in the rain.

II
We deluge upon each other, my head tilted up,
Myself the quenched. You a liquid taste,
Cool and studied like a vaporized Welsh spirit.

Let my rainfall move bodies with soak once more.
We're inundated by fountainlight. Hurry, inside.

III
Never mind the trance of your perfume
Or exact transcriptions of night declarations:
"I think I'm falling in love with you."

Never mind what our eyes do,
Especially symmetrical bedstares.

IV

Here I stand, an impossible man
Impossible to stand. I imagine you can't.
I throne myself for time enough to direct.

Gamely you perform, perhaps for art's sake,
For the sake of something that could last.

V

Restitch, O Winter Comforter,
Hurrying ahead of me,
Blowing kisses towards the lens.

The camera loves you to death
And so do I. So do I.

IT'S A JUDGMENT

Part the two flowering palmfronds
To an American paradise choking itself
With condensations of fogged-up desires.

Welcome. The pool is sterile and blue.
Dry off your diamonds, your whimpering
    companion.
All he wants is your body, still and soaking.
    Deny him.

Throw your clothes in the fire at nighttime,
    garment by garment.
The lights will always bring their colors through
    the window.
If you can't sleep, call the desk. They'll send one
    of the help along.

*Watching baseball in underwear, or rather just
    listening;
Reading a long book with a beer, two beers
One room but small, small enough for two.*

THE MESSAGE THEY TOOK
For Nicole

I don't want this to sound like an elegy
But they said you can't come to the phone right now
So, naturally, I'm concerned.
I've been imagining you as I knew you,
Dressed in that bizarre black kimono
With a rose across its back
And a red ballpoint through the bun
Of your dark Lebanese hair.
You speak perfect English.
And yet you have an extra door
And an extra lock
To walk through to go to bed.
I wondered why.
We talked about visiting all the states
Even bright Hawaii
Wild medication visions of shitty vans
And our tears as we listened to *Songs of Love
 and Hate*
Sprang to mind—
Anyway
I hope you're well

I saw you helpless

I saw you brave and wild

And you called me wise and beautiful

Close to my face

And how could I be any more poetic than that?

What could I possibly say?

I love you, but maybe you don't remember.

I don't think I'll call again.

Take care.

This is Rob, if you forget.

STREET WASH

See the girl. The only one of her kind in a group of four making their way down glistening Manhattan after the rain. A density to the smell rising from the nighttime pavement, a jostling sensation of direction and step. Nothing comes as a surprise to her anymore, save the thoughts of herself: for they, ever erratic and mechanized to bend perception into intrigue, were met with quizzical eyes from the city, left alone with the hovering scent of misunderstanding, trailing a straight line in the opposite direction.

Of the three men, she had only been to bed with the one. Call him Peter. He was older by nearly ten years and she had no qualm about that. She, at the back end of this small rhombus pack of bodies, could see his face at the front, craning itself up towards higher windows as he led himself through an exuberant rush of an anecdote, told with urgency and volume, though her mind allocated no space for its words to make themselves clear to her. All was muffled save for the sharper hush of the cruising traffic. He was laughing with abandon, perhaps hoping his voice would be carried by buildingsides down the funnel of the street and out to other boroughs where it could lift the heads of the less fortunate, the less educated. Perhaps it would teach them something about living.

Before she could find other corners in which she could hide her attention, they turned into a bar. Out flew a music that went on in its clean razorlike sound. A handsome Latino bartender in a bow tie, eyeing patrons with a resonant vacancy to his face. Lights that took the darkness in their arms, tightly, creating a haze of stimulant hues that cannot be found in nature. The faces were uniform in their open mid-conversation mouths, turned upwards in a hard interactivity, all facing one another at once. The drinks, even the beers, had a high-range smell that seemed itself an aesthetic choice, suited to this atmosphere of a clean, solid future away from things that can stain clothing.

Her mind now a field, green and to a fogged horizon on which the imagination could paint itself. A crown of trees surrounding it in a horseshoe. A boy she once knew down to the imperfections of his bones, pressing a flushed leaf in a journal into which she had intoned her simplest, heaviest wishes surreptitiously while he lay sleeping. She cannot remember what was written.

Her arm taken up now by Peter, who was close to her face shouting his breathless lust pride across it. His musk now with a stinging element, irritating. Like a child she felt herself pooling with what seemed a petulant discomfort against the sounds and the movement, and his smell. She felt him erect against her thigh and felt nothing else for the persisting moments that followed. A clear, almost crystalline drink made its way across her tongue and into her throat.

His apartment was dark with echoes of the bar. His girlfriend of two years and more was away for some kind of something he had described with incongruent words, disjunctive sentences that ended without conclusion. He made noise of the things he wanted to feel.

She was standing by the window and its good view of streets and lights, thinking of the boy asking a question while leaning over her. Her bedroom in a different place. How he'd moved over to the door. She turned on the conical lamp on the nightstand.

He turned a switch on the wall and the overhead light went out, covering his figure with a soft black to which the small shaded lamp could not extend its amber light. When he stepped into its circumference, a small arena of visibility, he was unclothed entirely for the first time for her. She, too, was undone save for a face she wore with a placidity that matched her fascination. The hair on his body shaped itself into patterns she studied for as long as he stood there, himself unable to move for the same feeling. Suddenly, she realized she was sleepy.

Here and now. Peter made little show of tenderness, but efforted his way down her concavities, lifting her left arm out of his way. The irritant of his smell persisted all across her in hovering vapor trails she traced in her recollections of where his head had been. They spiraled around her nakedness, with thicker clouds at her breasts, her hips, and one concentrated waft next to her head that fed itself in through her open pores.

Once she had driven hundreds of miles to see someone else. This one, Peter, was just downtown. She drew the map to his place in her head as she sat on the pillow next to him. All the linens seemed dingy. The dull edges of all thoughts and sensory irritants pelted themselves against the pale body, and by the time she blinked again she was longing for something much sharper.

Down the street again in the morning and at a pace enviable to those who actually had places to be, though she, covered in her nighttime film, her membrane that deflected sense, the embryo in which she had been incubating all this time, pushed forward without obligation save one that she demanded of herself, that is home and to quiet places without making conversation for all the effort it takes to put forward even a single string of phrases, especially those that could gather in her malcontent for purposes of repackaging in a way that would allow others to understand and act to rescue. No, she wanted no such thing save pity. Not even pity. Not pity.

CRYSTAL MADE FLESH

The hot winter hearts of the girls dive
Like young owls from the barn
Howling starblind against crowdfires
Into vacancies of the forest, snowed in.

Listen—the liquid arias of desperate men
Rise in an arc above the wholesale city nighttime
Over the graves of the impoverished
And hot streaks of futures passing.

They wail in breakneck Spanish
Quiero pasar la noche contigo
Into the forest aglow with January heartbeats.

THE RESOLUTION SEQUENCE

I

Give me one hour of lightless abandon:
I can engage with death's coiling, fingernailed form
All over my skinny boy back.

Let's burn our lengthening incense sticks of longing
And occupy each body inch of each other with pagan perfume
Until the air of our capsule smells like Miami.

And our lower Edens
Of which we are the tallest trees
Drive stick-shift into brackish rainforest fog—

For once I can look at you
And not even attempt an understanding
Beyond *you look so beautiful* in a travelled winter voice.

II

"How quickly," I wrote to a friend,
"You repair yourself with intimations of love!"
This was in a journal, in an alleyway.

And now I find myself aloft
Drizzled with the crudest human oils,
Being fish-cleaned by the barbs of longest
    eyelashes.

Through the caverns of my head canals
Rush elastic echoes of hollow moonlight past,
Hollow memories of gutting given a rounded
    high voice.

I turn to the caverns of birdcalls, behind
I wander in zigzags to a swift, soft departure
The exit gives way to caverns anew.

III

The thickest brush of neurons surrounds me.
The most earnest of cerebral worship
    surrounds me.
Surrounded, I forfeit my gray, mirrored blade.

Measure my brain from refractions of gray
Gray sheets absorbed by assemblies of bones
Bleachings of a body infused with my rain.

Measure your rain from alcoves above
Shallow alcoves giving way to earthcarvings
Carving divots with two animate pearls, or dewdrops.

I've tasted those dewdrops
They taste like mint
And grayscale.

IV

An assembly of heroes, an assembly of death
An assembly of grief, broadcast aloft
From the standing spire of a sunken minaret.

One hero tells me red is the color of the human soul
While another colors in the empty bellies of
    human hate,
His crimson palette quivering in veined hands.

Their capsule gives way to your building
Your building spills the reports of my body
Your shadow is still down there, scrubbing away.

And you cradle a bundle of neutral-gray fabric
With the approximate weight and radiant heat of
    a fawn
Rescued at last from a deepening future.

V
My immodest womanly weariness
Rushes to the rings around my dewdrops.
The brain, in light, gives way to inflammation.

You yank my gaze
As if it were a fasting horse
Deep in its godfaced march to true north.

My heroes
With their strange maverick routines
Grow old.

VI
May the fog of your apathy one day lift altogether,
So that we may see once more.
May your body fortify against the unwinding
    scroll,
The slack of which gathers at our ankles.
May the fawn remain precisely where it is,
Outside of time.

I SLEEP WITH SPIRITS

I sleep with spirits
I give them my body
But they do not take it.

Like northern winds the spirits swirl
In and around one another.
Their cold is my cold.

Like vapor the spirits move through me.
They move through musical instruments.
This is how we speak.

Real words would come
If I could move myself to stand.
The spirits do not untie me.

I study their orchestrations
They study my own
As if I were a calculating boy.

All I am is a boy
All I do is build great chains
The spirits, they just polish the links.

I don't sleep with the spirits,
The spirits sleep with me.

I long to be air.
I long to blow through you.
I long for you. I long for you now.

COVERINGS

The people enter and pass like bag drips, held aloft,
Leaving a chemical grief upon the tongue.

The blonde terrors, wandering the lawn,
Send guttural speech to the darkness.

We're listing out of time, we know;
All our hearts in vertigo.

You stumble once, fall into a snowbank
That feels, for a moment, like your mother's arms.

I enter, wearing a black hood, and ask myself
If I'd like my belongings sent ahead.

THEORY OF LIGHT

The sun was not strong, and yet it was forthright in its coming through that window and being just itself on the floor and in the air. It made us look honest.

The man at the front of the room spoke in a Missouri academia as he drew cartoon figures of the newborn and the middle-aged. They were, both of them, meant to be of his great aunt Hortense, whom he had known as the old woman of 1975: once, she'd left her false teeth under the bed at his parents' house during a visit, and after turning around and doubling the four hours of distance she had clocked from the split-level on Sycamore, she returned to the same bed that had belonged to the drowned brother while he lived. The bed was narrow, small. She slept with her teeth in.

I could sense a wealth of all knowledge from the affability of their smiles, the drawings. Next to each, the man drew midair spokes of a crude, oblique, darkaged wheel without circumference, and at the core of it was the word "soul," written out.

Could the baby girl, wrapped in an elliptical bundle with its single strand of hair sticking up, double-curlicued, be the same as the middle-aged mother across the way? Bespectacled, she too was smiling. Her hair ran up and over her crown in curls, ear to ear. He drew a dotted line from one being to the next. They are one and the same, he said.

The cold air of decaying dawn punctured us in all places. We will hide from it together, in bundles. The smiles from the front, just whiteboard smiles, held a warmth all their own. You will survive, they told us. Look at the light. Isn't it so beautiful?

THE PILGRIM

I am four hundred years an American.
Samuel Fuller, the doctor, couldn't save himself
From New World fever.
Could he save us from cancer?
No more than Eliot could, as I'd once believed.
Could I stop an aneurysm with a word?
I forget all my words. I could not.

Was there a seat at the First Thanksgiving table?
Doctor Fuller joined the hunters in the bird chase.
His fever could cook the cleaned birdflesh.
He was a godly man, according to neighbors.
Spring 1934: his deeper son, in a coal town,
Shoots his first rabbit, age six,
And will never handle a weapon again.
Today he is seated in perpetual autumn, now
    stately and old
At the table, a perfect sequoia circle,
A circular table without a head.
Here I sit, fasting with the democratized dead.
Together we starve to nothing.
Together we celebrate our Puritan cleanse.

Samuel tended to the retching stomachs of the
   Mayflower
He soaked rags in Plymouth freshwater for the
   diseased
And the vessel *Anne* carried dear Bridget after
   three years of unknown.
Myself, after just eight weeks tasting that rust of
   longing,
Caught sweet quiet tears on shirtsleeves,
Leaning on a tiled pillar under 116th Street.
I saw your face against the blur of an express train.
He saw hers descending upon America
From the wooden English bridge.

I could not save you, First Love,
From starvation.
I wanted you to sit beside me.
Second Love, I've ruined you.
I am that same fevered doctor
Using seventeenth-century surgery
To carry you on. I get sicker
And surely you wonder why.

A barge, it seems
Would be the best way to float
All our pregnant questions,

But let me carve canoes for each.
Let them slide down damways apart.
Let them find the Susquehanna caves.

There lies Thomas Morton
On a slab of slippery granite deep within the ground.
He wrote it down that the doctor
Ought to be led in parade down those muddy paths
Of a forgotten landscape called New Canaan
Upon a wild horse, with a necklace of Jurdans.
A quack, he called him.
I sentenced him to cave darkness
And he is the one who answers the questions I send.

Perhaps you call me the same, a quack
But I have no jurisdiction over those I love,
And you don't know the answers any more than I do.
At my lowest, I imagine you scooping out the rot
From those stuffed oak canoes.

I'm an explorer, eating space in the name of myself.
Burn me, convert me, Heathen of Love:
My bubbling young fervor wants to believe in you.
I'll clear a trail over hottest coals for the privilege,
For the honor,
And yet I spit wine like child's cake.

My god is one of inadvertent suffering,
Mistakes made with pillows and Lennie hands—
To think I had a purpose to things
Would be to think me too holy.
I am not holy. Neither are you.

So let us kiss the feet, the rings of others;
Explorers we are, disciples we hope to be.
Let us be blessed by familiar waters.
Let us architect a new, private America
Where the love is free and easy
Where the lust crashes in even waves
Where the words flow through touch.
Let us write out the cures for all death
And fail.

I was there
Fifteen minutes before, in a home bed.
That bed is now gone.
I was there
Fifteen minutes after, in a foreign bed
Fifteen minutes away from home.
That bed, occupied, remains.
We, the American living
Amongst the American dead,
Sit in waiting for you, feast untouched.

BEDSHEET LAMENT

It was torn when I awoke,
Classically musked and faded
Beneath my body, beached in slumber
And growing.

A tragedy, the desecration of something
Consecrated in the month of May,
In secret ceremony;
Nightmared, lustheaded—

I shouldered my own blame, thinking
I must have known what I was doing;
Tremoring arm reached in moonblue sleep,
Tremoring hand full of agesoft thread.

It should be burned, before an audience,
Not unlike the reverent pyre of a flag:
Longing in each curl of smoke.
Prayer in the ashes.

OLDER NOW

The porch is of deciduous wood from the forest
And it faces the pond. You sit,
Twilight-tired, in a homecarved rocking-chair.

One of your sons hurries past me,
Eyes fixed on you.
He has a daisy in his hand,
A daisy he fumbles and tucks into your hair.
He rocks you forwards, backwards.
He looks over at me. He doesn't know my name.
I smile a sad smile, and you call it a smile of age,
Happy and resigned.
It used to be we had to make sense of things like
  this,
Like you, your children, here and now, by the trees.

I step through a screen door to make fried eggs
  for everyone
With a grilled cheese on the side.
Your other son, he's young,
But he plays his gift guitar like a whisper.
He sits with it by the woodpile. You're playing
  tickle-tag with the other.

Through the window I can hear the melodies of
    your laughter
And the laugh of a melody, one string at a time.

At night, in my room, you tell me I should have some
Kids of my own. A daughter.
She and Mason can get married, you laugh.
I smile, your lamplit image flickering with tearwater,
Suspending itself. Another sign of age.

Everything smells like diffused woodsmoke
Except your skin, floral as if you'd been a
    wandering deer all day.
Exploring the meadows and eating the railroad lilies.
With your head on my shoulder, like a child, you
    ask for a story.
Your tired eyes point towards the baseboard. I
    look at the red in your hair,
And down at my hands, wrapped around one of
    yours.

Once there was a young man, I murmur,
Who found himself wandering forests in search
    of a place to lie down to die.
A finch hopped onto the path ahead and said
    nothing,

Sang a song that pulled him ahead.
A few miles and he emerged onto Fifth Avenue
Suddenly much older, and scanning the sidewalk
   for finches.

AXIOM

At the advent of his third and final love affair he thumbed back the cuff of his sleeve to find the time, which stared upwards to his face as an animal might; which told him something about the light; which had been shining upon the blondeness of a crown he hadn't yet touched with the symmetrical stretchings of hands. All days he would be surrounded, watching the wise girls adolesce as they listened to the dead singer prophets, the inarticulate hero boys they had imagined in the night with their exhumed and reembodied hands across bare abdomens, the fingers with their guitar callouses using muscles that music had stitched into them and them alone, the troubled and the gifted, the dead. They would dream of musician fingers in their mouths, one at a time, sucked clean.

Another such sequence involving walks to human monuments, Eiffel Towers in the winter morning, wool coats and cobblestones that glistened with the last evaporations of the city water from street hoses, a path of clean upon which they could tread with winged shoesoles. Only two such girls, so wise and so foolish indeed, had made him into such a hero, such a monument, a walking partner with hands. Perhaps they'd imagined him dead by now.

One of them, the first, remembered his tongue as the taste of plantmatter against hers. As if he had a bitter resonance and health, as if he had a medicinal value quantifiable by science in a way that would allow one to recommend him to her, perhaps flourish the sentiment with grand hyperbole, perhaps tell her that he was the kind that nourished life.

Histories were moments packed as foodtins, not quite factoried but manufactured by strokes of timing as if from a divine itinerary. He imagined his moves of love inscribed into stone as perverted Roman letters, caves full of these two loves past and those to come, extending far away from the mouth of light into old age, unreadable for all the dark and cold, awash in a forbidding air of cholera and rheumatic fever, ticks crawling across these tablets, bloated with the blood of the future.

When he entered the last hour of light with her, in the sort of winter stride that allowed for shoulders to kiss and depart at regular intervals of time, she remembered the letters she wrote on his skin not two months prior, a sea ago. The trees were thin with youth, birched by the paleness of the light. He took notice of her eyebrows: their thickness as he always would, lush and organic, dark with intrigue and expressive in a way she could not be for all her secrecy, hints at opaqueness and despair, love ruined, a smothering optimism for him. It was a history he would manufacture soon enough, for it seemed her eyes, her eyelashes beckoned to his imaginations.

Once, they had kept each other awake with kisses and bodystrokes until dawn, until he had to leave and she, in her bareness and light, felt the inauguration complete enough for him to go. He longed for inaugurations. He longed for her once more, and there she was.

Torn in two by two horses; two horses as two lives pointed to opposite seas; two favorable winds through beautiful auburn and amber manes, set alight with movement; two loves; two loves; a heart not of ventricles but of precious, resilient metals; kilnfires of emotion and molds of grief filled with the rainwater of a man's own making and hoisted above the head perhaps as a merchant would, or rather a prophet. The sun reflected itself from the glaze onto her face in a kind of rose, warm enough perhaps but certainly too bright, too strong a notion of love so as to turn one's head from the gift, the baptism of it all, arranged too quickly but without hesitation for lack of feeling. He loved her. He loved her dearly as one's own window landscape, not a sense of ownership but a sense of place and belonging so innate and anchoring. He is part of that picture, out to the lines of city architecture, windows dense with other lives, or to the kind of hills that dip like body sculpture and yield the very atmosphere of love and life from the greenery. His window will project whichever sight he pleases, and yet it is not his choice to make.

She was silent, made no indication that the future was of any concern. The dreams lingered, were filed away. She turned and smiled away from him, then her eyes drifted back to his face. How could anyone see his face with that kind of love? He began to search for caves, for his future underground. His eyes went over the wide forest, and the ground swelled open in several small places all along his line of sight.

HERE MY MIND

Here my mind,
Bereft of all consequence, like a ladybug;
A thing only made worthy through myth and
Mysticism, power as dubious as voodoo.

Here my mind,
Humming instrument of imagery, colorspots;
Something asymmetrical. Like a titanium scooter
That rolls down the hill carrying a loud child
Who goes silent after the crash, pulling the thing
Behind him while cradling a bleeding forearm.

Here my mind,
Waiting for other minds to fill it;
Something gray and always pacing around,
Exhausting itself with the effort. It eats the air
And look: a boy, a young man, a boy
With a flower in his ear, looking away from someone
Who will see him again as a demon in dreams,
As the lover of all her many angles:
The angle of sleeping in an old city house with her
The angle of facing a gray sea with her
The angle of turning the TV off against her

The angle of her in cities, views and skylines
Her against music and low light, against
Men born as men who sleep 200 miles closer to her.
A deep freeze of solitude. The mind has forgotten
How cold it can get, but the body knows.

Here my mind,
Running in the street like some
Afterword, nebulous and erect at the end
Of some fruitful tome of a novel;
All at once saying nothing about an answer
And still finding your heart deep in the breast
Cornered and throbbing, a singular bruise
That will make no appointments, speak to no
    audiences.
It holds the thing like a desperate lover while
Stringing along all the hyperboles of truth.

SESTINA FOR A PLATEAU

Normal people aren't patient for nearness
Their minds stick fast with grade-school colours
Like the adhesive fingerpaints of their daughters
Heavens, it's unconscionable to simply sit still
And close: Funny how the patient ones seem wild
One day they'll stick us in a cooped-up case.

Ours is affection, and a rather special case
Founded in a long-fermented nearness
Years enough to make us wild
Plenty of time to mix strange colours
I sometimes think we're mixing still
Like holiday cake being baked by daughters.

Do you still imagine my many daughters?
In my deepest visions it has never been the case
But I compile awful baby-names, even still
And hardly consider my astonishing nearness
To the age: reality will hit me with all its colours
Like a bunkered frustrated Van Gogh, gone wild.

Months ago I saw four dozen turkeys in the wild
Larger, fatter ones flanked by many daughters

Under a winter tree, among a field devoid of colours
My good fortune, I brought my camera just in case
But the shot was yards away, I longed for nearness
The thought of such a rare crowd haunts me still.

I'm one of those mad artist idealists, rarely still
Destined to end up rotten in the deep wild
Cities bother me, I balk at all the nearness
That's no place I'd raise my daughters
Unless chance gives me the means, an unusual case
Though I know opportunities come in many colours.

My memories of you drown all with their colours
They've always quenched these thoughts, even still
I'll pack them some day in an antique burgundy case
Finally hustle my way into the dark, emotional wild
Perhaps I'll emerge with a couple of daughters
My perfect pair: nothing earthly will rival our
    nearness.

And though my vision ahead is blurry
(I cannot see very far)
I can make out a raven-nymph on the horizon
Next to a frightfully skinny silhouette, stepping on.

INHERITANCE

Veronica.
Stitched with violet thread,
blue and red.

You stand at the still point,
waist deep, skirt soaking in the shallows.
Swanling. Veronica.

Such myopia. Intangible.
When I stretch my hands before me,
they soak in dissolution like it was a pool.

A hill, a highland. A bear watches you grow.
Away from the water, you encounter
a bird that says *pip*.

A room brimmed over with crystal sand.
A tangle of mercury cirrus ahead.
At your approach, it blossoms to flame.

The city in fury. You've arrived nonetheless.
I pale in the void of your sadness, my own.
You paint high flowers in quivering strokes.

Veronica, you
in your violets, your royal hues.
My noblesse. I bow at the sight of you.

All that I possess,
all words and anxieties,
I hereby bequeath.

In this world, we resign ourselves
at the end of our daylit meridian hustle
to the inky violets and blues of living.

My darling girl.
The world is wide as the length of a breath.
Birds erupting from the virgin breast.

You, standing at my vanishing point.
Buoyant, patient. The waiting room
is watertight. Yes. I promise.

I promise you. This is for you. You. Veronica.

Deep gratitude and acknowledgment to the following for their generous financial contribution to the publication of this collection, and without whom this book would be impossible:

    Christina Amen
    Kimberly Brown
    Christian Cassidy-Amstutz
    Zachary Cole
    Alex Cunningham
    Gail Fuller
    Judi Hummel
    Prairwa Leerasanthanah
    Elbert Mets
    Sarah Preston
    Sara Sajer
    Evan Spitzer
    Pamela Whitenack
    Naomi Zeigler

Robert S. Hummel was born in Hershey, Pennsylvania. He has written a variety of prose, poetry, stage plays, and screenplays. He also produces work in cinema and photography. He currently resides in Ithaca, NY.

r o b e r t s h u m m e l . c o m